TULSA CITY-COUNTY LIBRARY

MAR - - 2024

6 MASTER LEVEL PAPER AIRPLANES

BY JENNIFER SANDERSON

Express!

BELLWETHER MEDIA • MINNEAPOLIS, MN

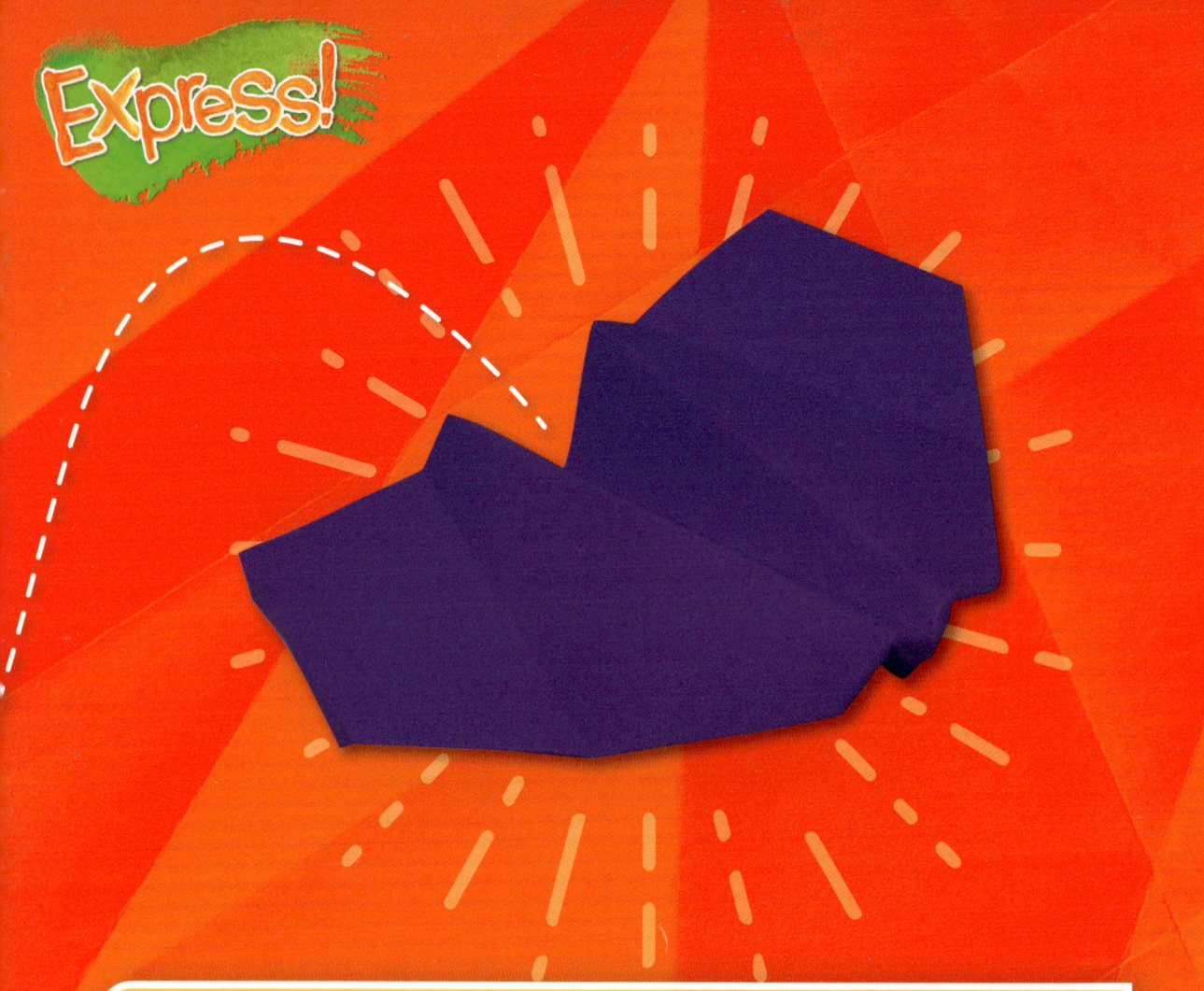

This edition first published in 2022 by Bellwether Media, Inc.

No part of this publication may be reproduced in whole or in part without written permission of the publisher. For information regarding permission, write to Bellwether Media, Inc., Attention: Permissions Department, 6012 Blue Circle Drive, Minnetonka, MN 55343.

Library of Congress Cataloging-in-Publication Data
Names: Sanderson, Jennifer, author.
Title: Master level paper airplanes / by Jennifer Sanderson.
Description: Minneapolis, MN : Bellwether Media, Inc., 2022. | Series: Express!: Take flight! | Includes bibliographical references and index. | Audience: Ages 7-13 | Audience: Grades 4-6 | Summary: "Step-by-step instructions inform how to fold various paper airplanes. The text level and subject matter are intended for students in grades 3 through 8" --Provided by publisher.
Identifiers: LCCN 2021021451 (print) | LCCN 2021021452 (ebook) | ISBN 9781644875575 (library binding) | ISBN 9781648344657 (ebook)
Subjects: LCSH: Paper airplanes--Juvenile literature.
Classification: LCC TL778 .S2627 2022 (print) | LCC TL778 (ebook) | DDC 745.592--dc23
LC record available at https://lccn.loc.gov/2021021451
LC ebook record available at https://lccn.loc.gov/2021021452

Text copyright © 2022 by Bellwether Media, Inc. EXPRESS and associated logos are trademarks and/or registered trademarks of Bellwether Media, Inc.

Editors: Elizabeth Neuenfeldt and Christina Leaf
Designers: Jeffery Kollock and Laura Sowers
Paper Engineer: Jessica Moon

Printed in the United States of America, North Mankato, MN.

TABLE OF CONTENTS

Making Planes	4
The Javelin	6
The Twister	8
Pinnacle	10
The Victory	12
Tuck and Glide	14
Fighter Plane	16
The Pointer	18
The Beast	20
Glossary	22
Tips	22
To Learn More	23
Index	24

MAKING PLANES

Most people have made a paper plane. They are easy to make and only require a sheet of paper. The Chinese were the first to make paper. They likely made flying objects from their paper.

In the late 1400s, Italian artist and inventor Leonardo da Vinci tested flying machines made with **parchment**. The Wright Brothers also used paper planes as tests before they took flight in 1903.

Paper planes were popular during **World War II**. Toys were hard to find. But paper was always available, so children made planes for fun. In this book, you can use **origami** techniques to fold eight different paper planes. Have fun!

ORIGAMI FOLDS

 **Valley fold** Lift the paper and bend it toward you.

 **Mountain fold** Bend the paper backward, away from you.

 **Pleat fold** First fold the paper in one direction, and then in the opposite direction.

 **Squash fold** Two layers open and are then squashed flat.

 **Inside reverse fold** Push the tip of the paper inward, then flatten.

ORIGAMI SYMBOLS

Below are key origami instruction symbols. You will find these throughout the book.

| Valley fold | Mountain fold | Pleat fold  | Cut line |

 Fold direction    Flip paper   Rotate paper

SUPPLIES

- Colorful paper
- Ruler or metal spoon for flattening folds
- Colored pencils and markers
- Glitter glue and other decorations
- Scissors

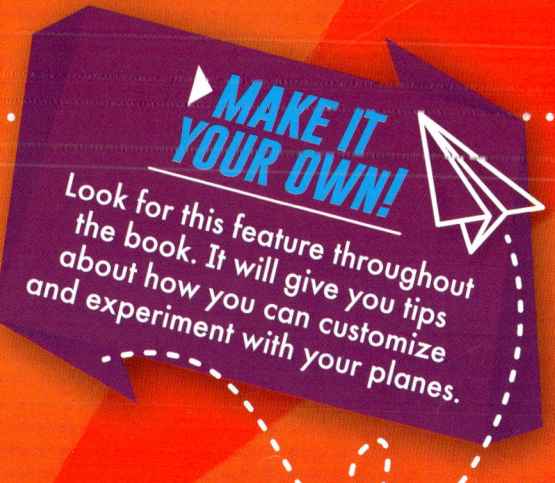

MAKE IT YOUR OWN! Look for this feature throughout the book. It will give you tips about how you can customize and experiment with your planes.

THE JAVELIN

Paper size
Sheet of paper approximately 8.5 x 11 inches (22 x 28 centimeters)

This **style** of paper airplane is made for speed. Watch it zip through the air!

1
Make a squash fold in the top square of your paper.

2
Valley fold up the upper triangles to the top.

3
Cut small slits in the bottom of your plane.

CUT   CUT

4
Mountain fold back the flaps you cut in Step 3.

SQUASH

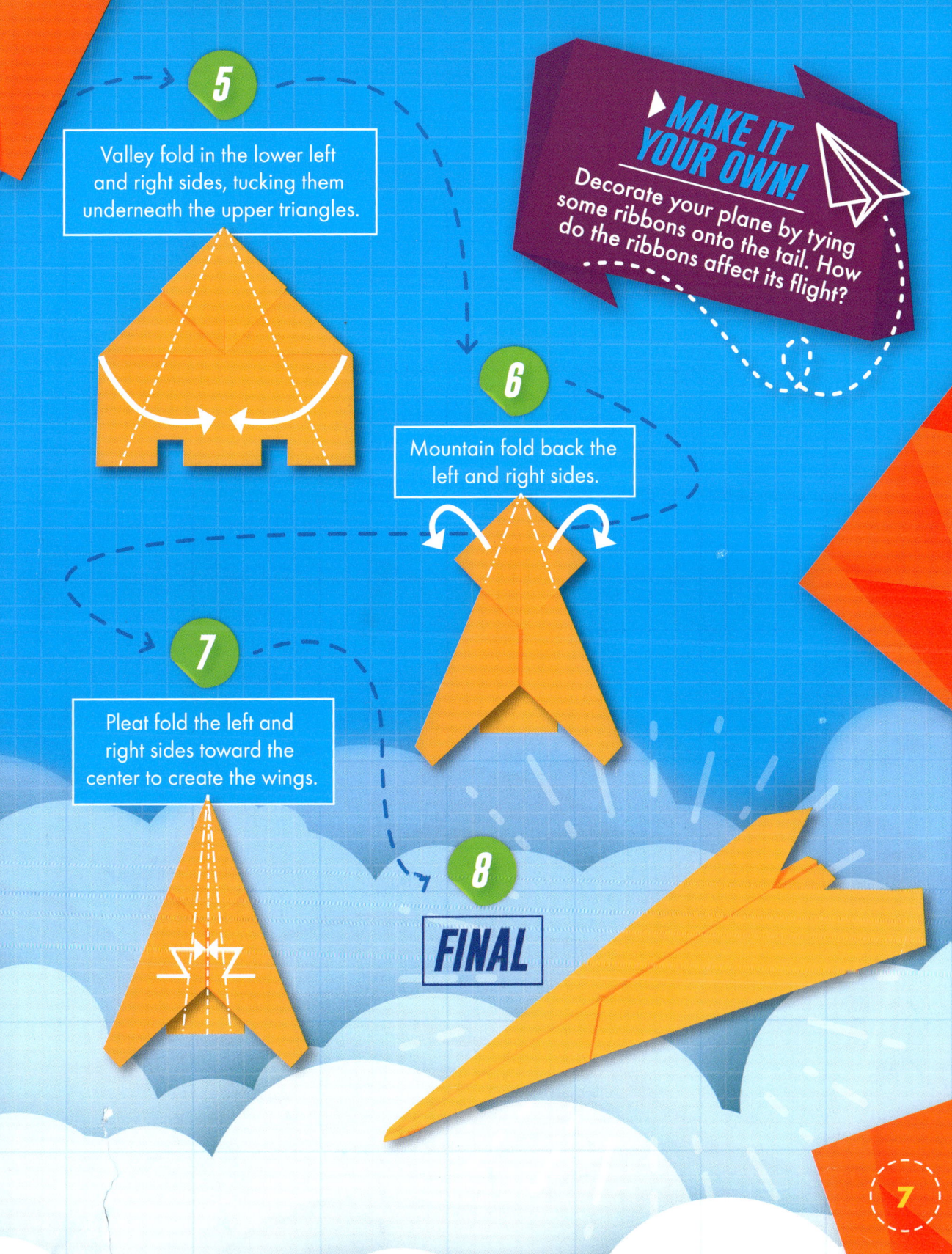

THE TWISTER

Paper size
Sheet of paper approximately 8.5 x 11 inches (22 x 28 centimeters)

The flaps and wings on this paper airplane help it stay in the air. See how well it flies!

1 Valley fold your paper in half both ways, and unfold it.

2 Valley fold in the top left and right sides to the center.

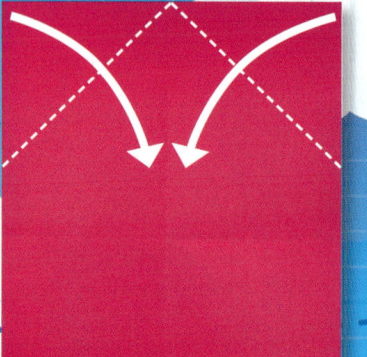

3 Valley fold in the left and right sides to the center again.

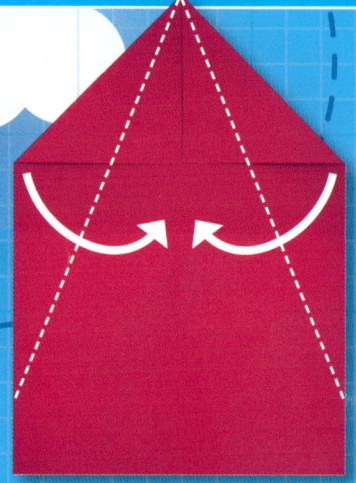

4 Mountain fold back the top.

5 Valley fold in the left and right sides to the center.

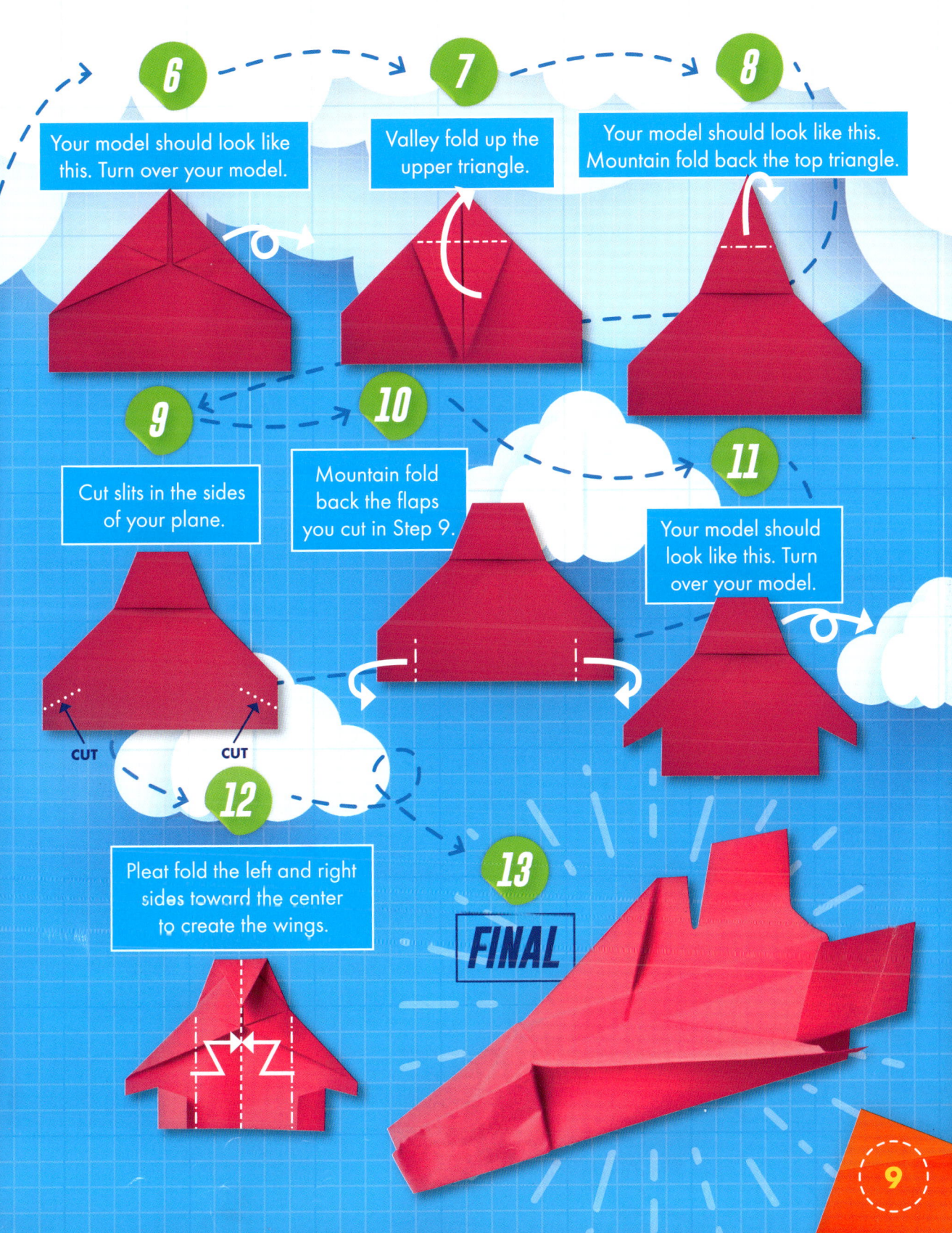

PINNACLE

Paper size
Sheet of square paper approximately 8 x 8 inches (20 x 20 centimeters)

Carefully follow each step to make this cool plane. Soon it will be ready to soar!

1 Valley fold your paper in half.

2 Valley fold down the top.

3 Cut slits in the sides of your plane.

CUT   CUT

4 Valley fold up the flaps you cut in Step 3.

10

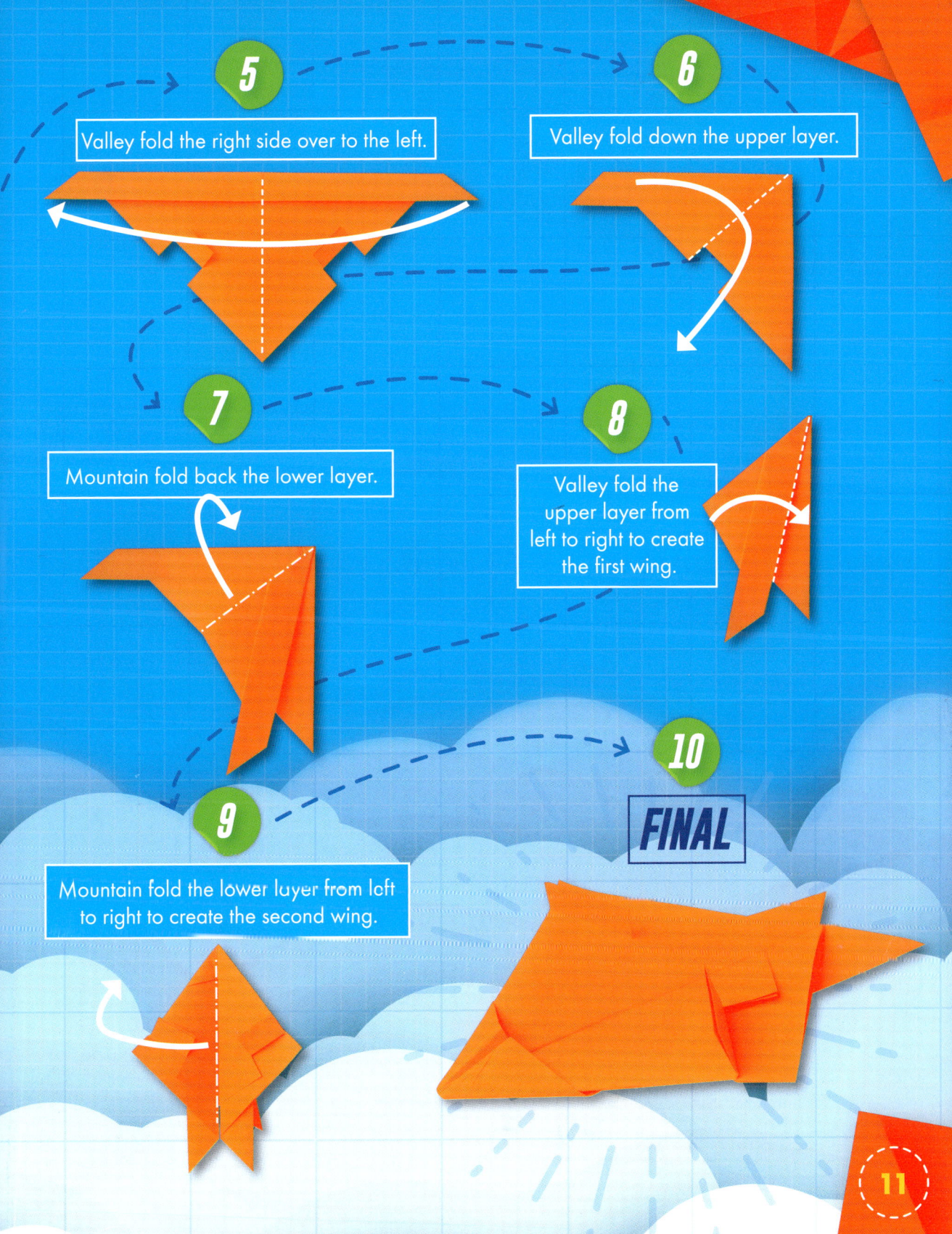

THE VICTORY

Paper size
Sheet of square paper approximately 8 x 8 inches (20 x 20 centimeters)

The wide wings on this paper airplane will help it go far. See how long it can stay in the air!

1 Valley fold your paper in half from left to right. Unfold it.

2 Valley fold in the top left and right sides to the center.

3 Valley fold down the top point.

4 Valley fold in the top left and right sides to the center.

12

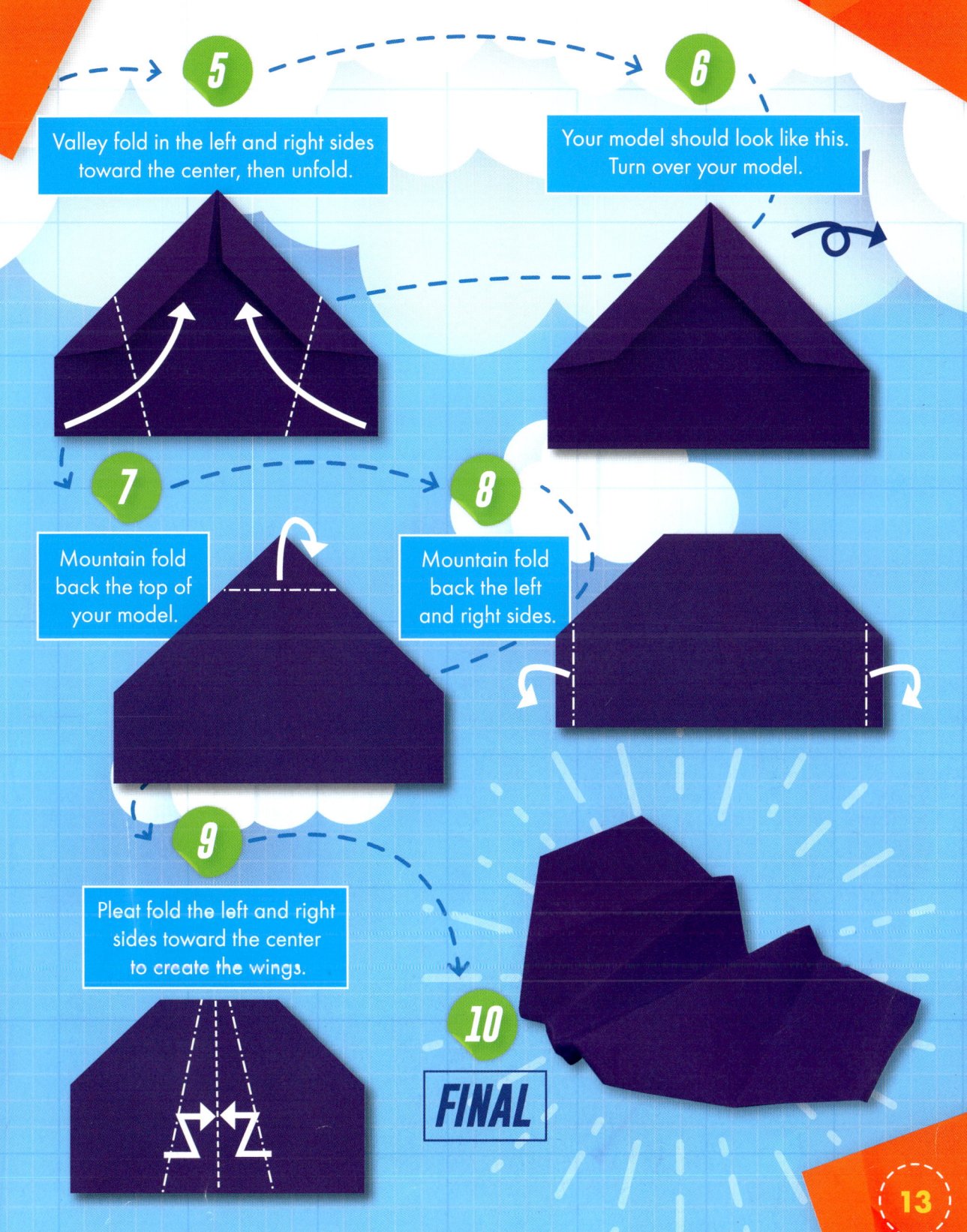

TUCK AND GLIDE

Paper size
Sheet of paper approximately 8.5 x 11 inches (22 x 28 centimeters)

This plane's **unique** shape gives it a steady flight through the air!

1 Make a squash fold in the top square of your paper.

SQUASH

2 Valley fold down the top.

3 Valley fold in the upper left and right triangles to the center.

4 Valley fold in the upper left and right triangles again, tucking them into the center triangle.

14

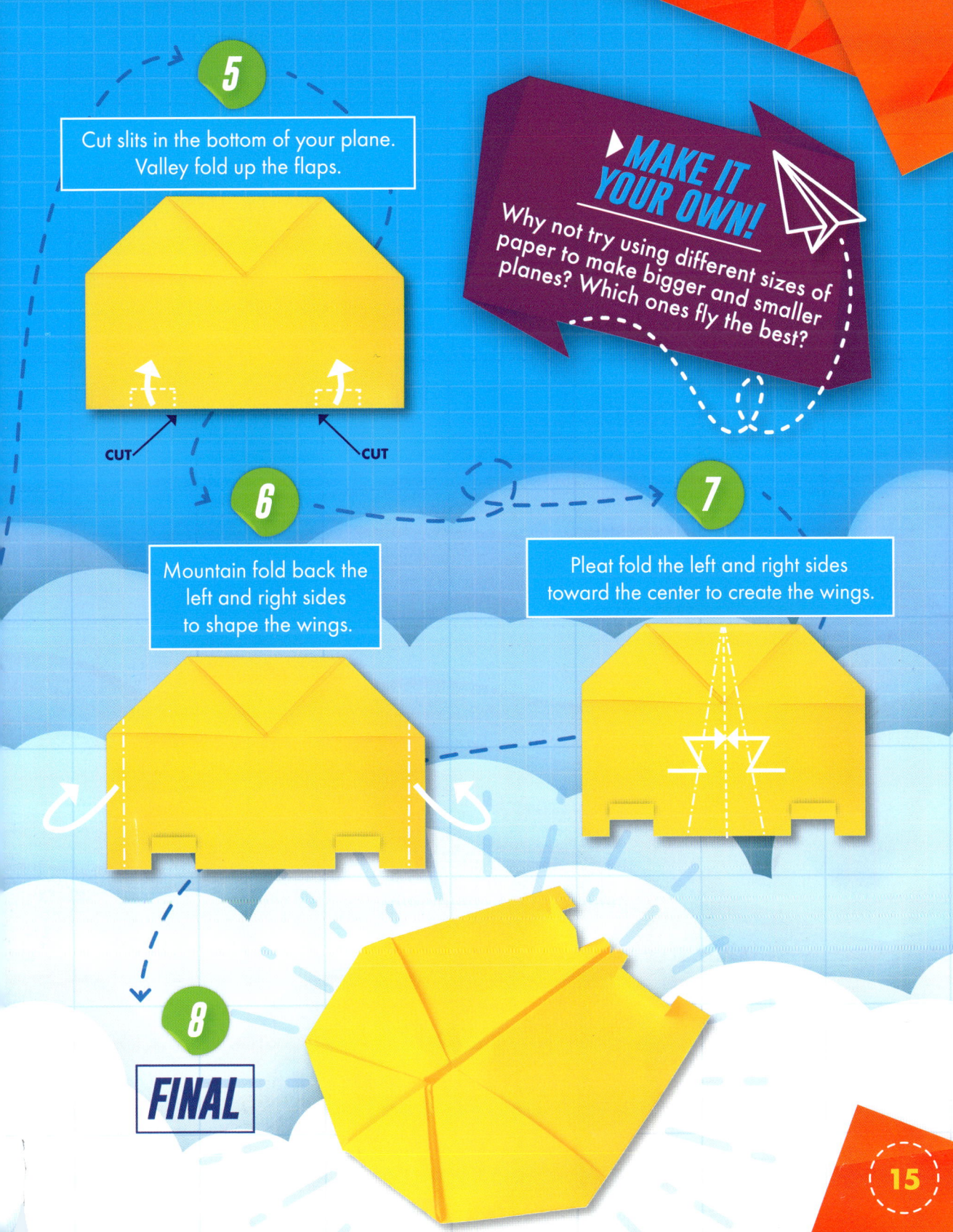

FIGHTER PLANE

Paper size
Sheet of paper approximately 8.5 x 11 inches (22 x 28 centimeters)

Modeled after fighter jets, this paper airplane is ready to take control of the skies!

1 Valley fold your paper in half along the long side, and then unfold it.

2 Valley fold in the top left and right sides to the center.

3 Valley fold down the top left edge to the bottom left edge, then unfold.

4 Valley fold down the top right edge to the bottom right edge, then unfold.

16

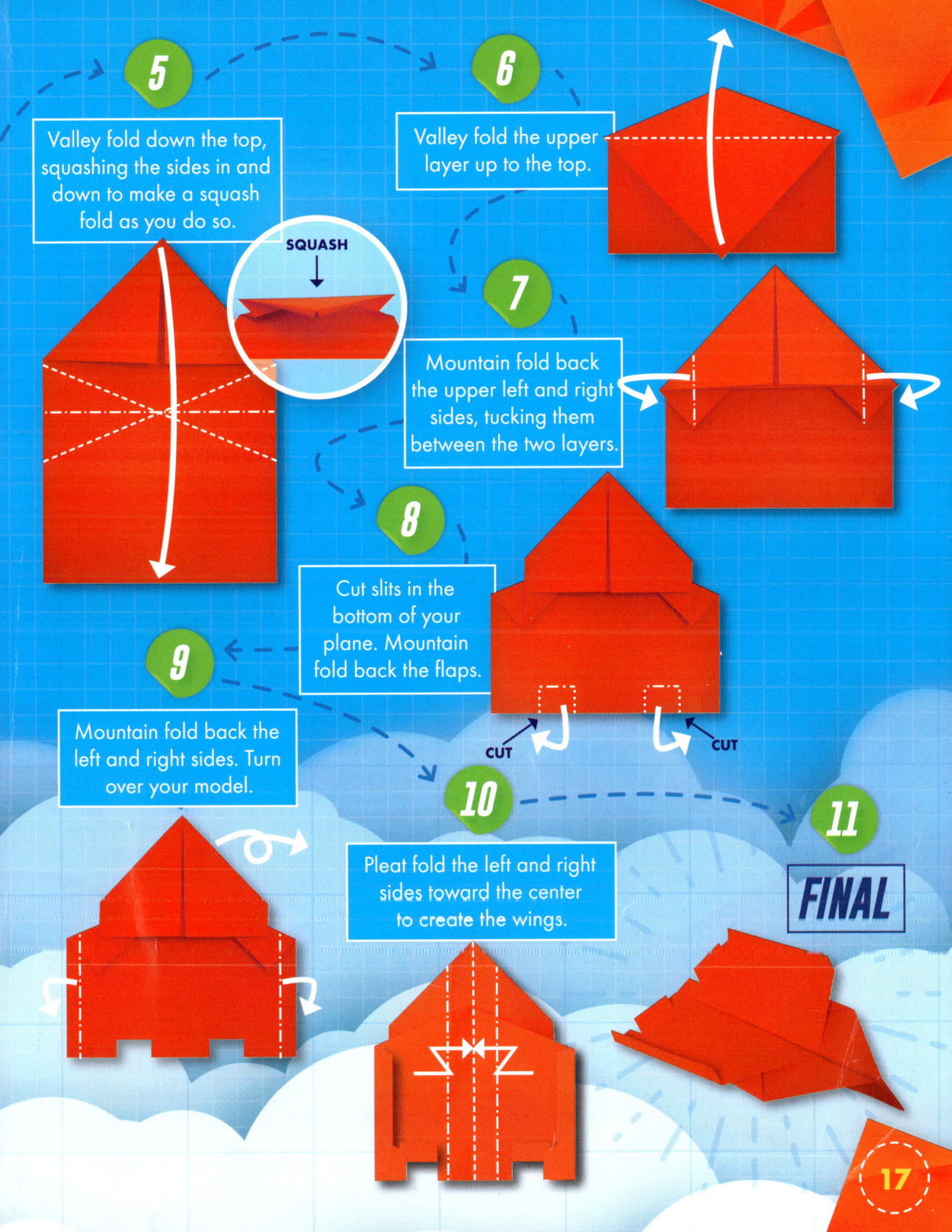

THE POINTER

Paper size
Sheet of paper approximately 8.5 x 11 inches (22 x 28 centimeters)

The narrow shape of this paper airplane will help it zoom through the air. Try it out!

1 Valley fold your paper in half, and then unfold it.

2 Valley fold in the top left and right sides to the center.

3 Valley fold in the top left and right sides to the center.

4 Valley fold in the left and right sides to the center again.

5 Your model should look like this. Open your model so it looks like it did at the end of Step 2.

OPEN   OPEN

18

THE BEAST

Paper size
Sheet of paper approximately 8.5 x 11 inches (22 x 28 centimeters)

This paper airplane stands out with its unusual shape. See how it flies!

1 Make a squash fold in the top square of your paper.

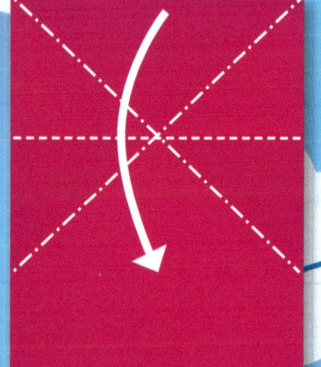

2 Valley fold in the upper left and right triangles to the center.

3 Valley fold down the upper triangle top layer.

4 Valley fold in the bottom left and right sides of the diamond shape, and then unfold.

5 Valley fold in the top left and right sides of the diamond shape, and then unfold.

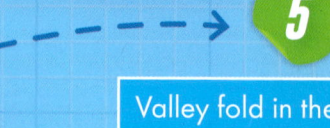

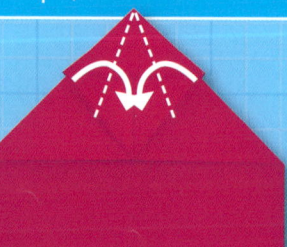

20

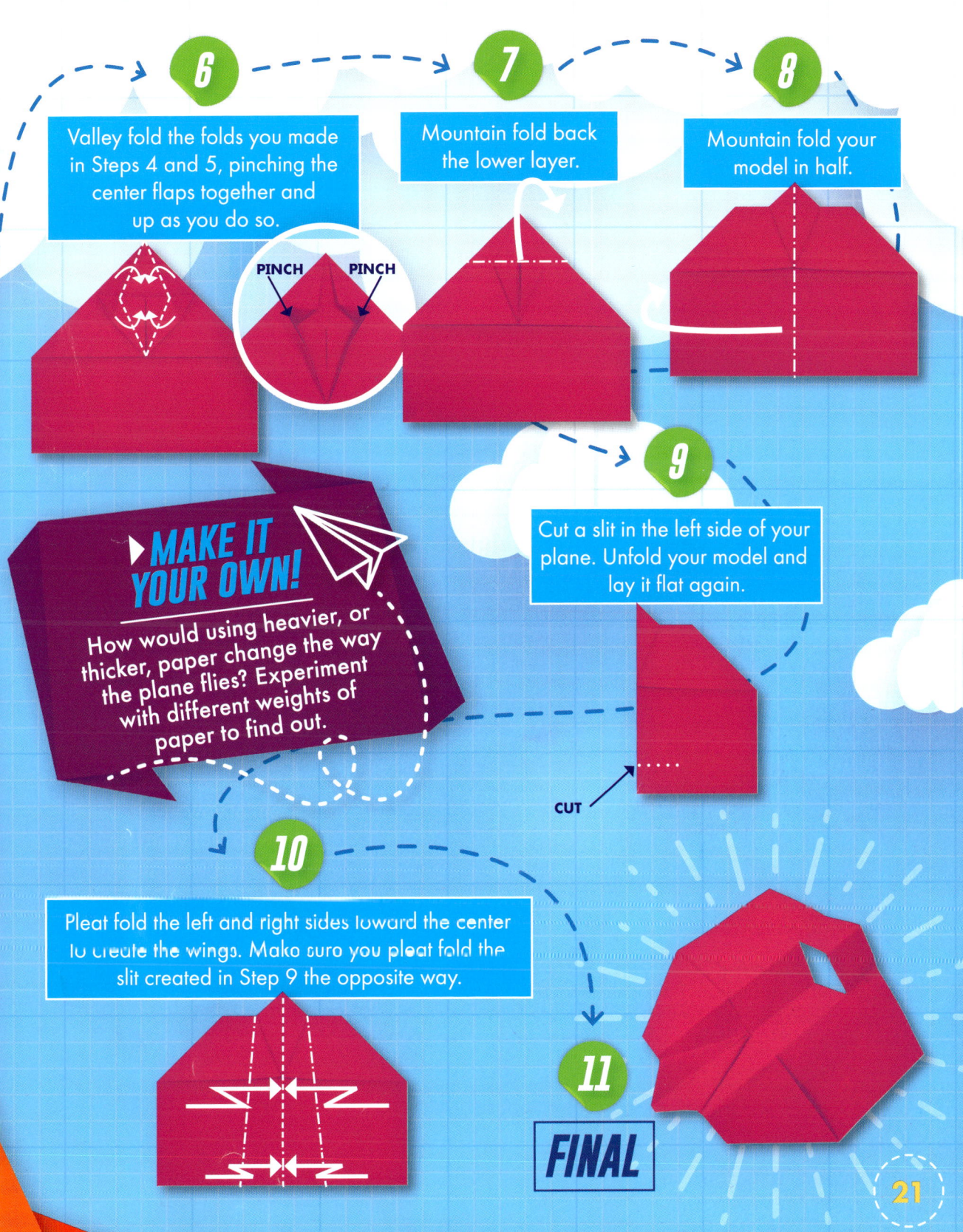

GLOSSARY

origami—the Japanese art of paper folding

parchment—paper made from animal skins

style—a distinct form

unique—one of a kind

World War II—the war fought from 1939 to 1945 that involved many countries

TIPS

▸ Always look ahead to the next step to see where you are going.

▸ Make a soft crease in the paper. Make sure it is in the right place before you press down hard to make a sharp crease.

▸ If you make a big mistake when you fold, recycle the paper and start over. A fold in the wrong place can throw your plane out of balance!

▸ Practice making your favorite paper planes. In no time, you will get better and better! Try making your favorite airplane a few times. It will be easier each time!

TO LEARN MORE

AT THE LIBRARY

Hardyman, Robyn. *Aircraft*. Minneapolis, Minn.: Bellwether Media, 2018.

Merrill, Jayson. *Easy Aircraft Origami: 14 Cool Paper Projects Take Flight*. Mineola, N.Y.: Dover Publications, Inc., 2020.

Oachs, Emily Rose. *The Airplane*. Minneapolis, Minn.: Bellwether Media, 2019.

ON THE WEB

FACTSURFER

Factsurfer.com gives you a safe, fun way to find more information.

1. Go to www.factsurfer.com.

2. Enter "paper airplanes" into the search box and click 🔍.

3. Select your book cover to see a list of related content.

INDEX

beast, 20-21
Chinese, 4
da Vinci, Leonardo, 4
fighter plane, 16-17
history, 4
javelin, 6-7
make it your own, 5, 7, 15, 21
pinnacle, 10-11
pointer, 18-19
supplies, 5
techniques, 4, 5
tuck and glide, 14-15
twister, 8-9
victory, 12-13
World War II, 4
Wright Brothers, 4